W9-ALI-218

OFFICIALLY
WITHDRAWN

A Beginning-to-Read Book

Dear Dragon Goes to the Aquarium

by Margaret Hillert

Illustrated by Jack Pullan

NORWOOD HOUSE PRESS

DEAR CAREGIVER, The *Beginning-to-Read* series is a carefully written collection of classic readers you may remember from your own childhood. Each book features text comprised of common sight words to provide your child ample practice reading the words that appear most frequently in written text. The many additional details in the pictures enhance the story and offer the opportunity for you to help your child expand oral language and develop comprehension.

Begin by reading the story to your child, followed by letting him or her read familiar words and soon your child will be able to read the story independently. At each step of the way, be sure to praise your reader's efforts to build his or her confidence as an independent reader. Discuss the pictures and encourage your child to make connections between the story and his or her own life. At the end of the story, you will find reading activities and a word list that will help your child practice and strengthen beginning reading skills.

Above all, the most important part of the reading experience is to have fun and enjoy it!

Shannon Cannon

Shannon Cannon, Ph.D.
Literacy Consultant

Norwood House Press • P.O. Box 316598 • Chicago, Illinois 60631
For more information about Norwood House Press please visit our website at *www.norwoodhousepress.com* or call 866-565-2900.

LIBRARY OF CONGRESS CATALOGING-IN-PUBLICATION DATA
Hillert, Margaret.
Dear Dragon goes to the aquarium / by Margaret Hillert ; illustrated by Jack Pullan.
pages cm. -- (A Beginning-to-read book)
Summary: "A boy and his pet dragon go on a field trip to the aquarium. They see several fish and other animals that live in the water. This title includes reading activities and a word list"-- Provided by publisher.
ISBN 978-1-59953-677-4 (library edition : alk. paper) -- ISBN 978-1-60357-737-3 (ebook)
[1. Aquariums--Fiction. 2. Dragons--Fiction.] I. Pullan, Jack, illustrator. II. Title.
PZ7.H558Deap 2015
[E]--dc23
2014030279

262N—122014
Manufactured in the United States of America in North Mankato, Minnesota.

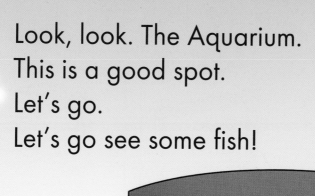

Look, look. The Aquarium.
This is a good spot.
Let's go.
Let's go see some fish!

Come look at this.
There are lots of fish.
Some big.
Some small.
Let's go see more!

This is a sea turtle.
It is big, big, big.
Now let's see some horses!

Horses? No, no.
We will not see horses.
This is an aquarium!

Oh yes, I see.
I see little, little sea horses.

Oh, oh!
This is not a fish.
How many legs do you see?

There is a cat here, too.

A cat? No, no. No cat.
This is an aquarium!

Look, look!
See a fish that looks like a cat?
A cat fish!

Oh, oh, oh!
This fish has a lot of teeth.
That is not good.

Now let's look for a clown.

No, no.
There are no clowns.
This is an aquarium!

I see the clown.
It is a clown fish.
It is not funny.
It is pretty, pretty, pretty.

17

But, here are some funny birds.
They walk funny.

Now let's look at the stars!

No, no. There are no stars here.
This is an aquarium!

Look at this one—
and this one—
and this one.
Star fish!

Look at these fish.
They like to play.

Now let's look for gold!

No, no.
There is no gold here.
This is an aquarium!

Oh, I see.
I see gold fish!

That was fun,
but now it is time to go home.

Here I am with you.
Here you are with me.
Oh what a good day, Dear Dragon!

READING REINFORCEMENT

The following activities support the findings of the National Reading Panel that determined the most effective components for reading instruction are: Phonemic Awareness, Phonics, Vocabulary, Fluency, and Text Comprehension.

Phonemic Awareness: The /a/ sound

1. Say the word **apple** and ask your child to repeat the beginning sound. Say the word **can** and ask your child to repeat the middle sound. Say it slowly to help your child identify the middle /**a**/ sound.

2. Explain to your child that you are going to say some words and you would like her/him to give you a thumbs-up if s/he hears the short /**a**/ as in apple or can, or a thumbs-down if it is not the short /**a**/ sound.

ate (↓)	at (↑)	cap (↑)	cape (↓)
mat (↑)	mate (↓)	and (↑)	van (↑)
sad (↑)	sand (↑)	grass (↑)	game (↓)

Phonics: Word Ladder

Word ladders are a fun way to build words by changing just one letter at a time. Write the word **ark** on a piece of paper and give your child the following step-by-step instructions (the letters between the / / marks indicate that you are to give the sound as a clue rather than providing the actual letter):

- Add the /**b**/ sound to the beginning of the word. What do you have? (**bark**)
- Change the /**k**/ to a /**n**/. What do you have? (**barn**)
- Change the /**b**/ to a /**y**/. What do you have? (**yarn**)
- Change the /**n**/ to a /**d**/. What do you have? (**yard**)
- Change the /**y**/ to a /**c**/. What do you have? (**card**)
- Change the /**d**/ to a /**t**/. What do you have? (**cart**)

Vocabulary: Story-related Words

1. Write the following words on sticky note paper and point to them as you read them to your child:

fish	turtle	horse	cat
clown	star	gold	bird

2. Mix the words up. Say each word in random order and ask your child to point to the correct word as you say it.

3. Mix the words up again and ask your child to read as many as he or she can.

4. Ask your child to place the notes on the correct page for each word, i.e. **turtle** goes on the page turtles are talked about.

Fluency: Choral Reading

1. Reread the story with your child at least two more times while your child tracks the print by running a finger under the words as they are read. Ask your child to read the words he or she knows with you.

2. Reread the story aloud together. Be careful to read at a rate that your child can keep up with.

3. Repeat choral reading and allow your child to be the lead reader and ask him or her to change from a whisper to a loud voice while you follow along and change your voice.

Text Comprehension: Discussion Time

1. Ask your child to retell the sequence of events in the story.

2. To check comprehension, ask your child the following questions:

   • How many legs does the animal on page 10 have?

   • Do you know what fish is pictured on page 14 and has a lot of teeth?

   • Have you ever been to the Aquarium? What was your favorite fish?

WORD LIST

Dear Dragon Goes to the Aquarium uses the 74 words listed below.

The **9** words bolded below serve as an introduction to new vocabulary, while the other 65 are pre-primer. You may wish to write the words on index cards and use them to help your child build automatic word recognition. Regular practice with these words will enhance your child's fluency in reading connected text.

a	fish	**legs**	**sea**	walk
am	for	let's	see	was
an	fun	like	small	we
and	funny	little	some	what
aquarium		look(s)	spot	will
are	go	lot(s)	**star(s)**	with
at	**gold**			
	good	many	**teeth**	yes
big		me	that	you
birds	has	**more**	the	
but	here		there	
	home	no	these	
cat	horses	not	they	
clown(s)	how	now	this	
come			time	
	I	of	to	
day	is	oh	too	
dear	it	one	**turtle**	
do				
dragon		play		
		pretty		

ABOUT THE AUTHOR Margaret Hillert has written over 80 books for children who are just learning to read. Her books have been translated into many different languages and over a million children throughout the world have read her books. She first started writing poetry as a child and has continued to write for children and adults throughout her life. A first grade teacher for 34 years, Margaret is now retired from teaching and lives in Michigan where she likes to write, take walks in the morning, and care for her three cats.

Photograph by Glenna Washburn

ABOUT THE ILLUSTRATOR A talented and creative illustrator, Jack Pullan, is a graduate of William Jewell College. He has also studied informally at Oxford University and the Kansas City Art Institute. He was mentored by the renowned watercolor artists, Jim Hamil and Bill Amend. Jack's work has graced the pages of many enjoyable children's books, various educational materials, cartoon strips, as well as many greeting cards. Jack currently resides in Kansas.